MW00932604

Interface
2018

MARIA KABANOVA

ILLUSTRATED BY MARGARITA GREZINA

LITTLE MONSTRIE'S BIG ADVENTURES

WHO IS MONSTRIE?

READ ON TO FIND OUT!

Little Monstrie's Big Adventures

Come and join little Monstrie's adventures! He's sometimes shy – but sometimes brave and daring. He tames a firebird, stands up to bullies, sets out to save his mum from gangsters, starts a growl band, and even solves the great Monster School mystery!

These stories are about friendship, kindness, and the courage needed to be true to yourself.

Check out Monstrie's fun games and competitions at: www.monstrie.com

By Maria Kabanova

Translated by the author
Illustrations and book design by Margarita Grezina
Edited by Karen Atkinson at Karen Atkinson Editorial and Sarah Stewart at Lighthouse Literary

First Published 2018 by Interface

ISBN 978-5-6041013-0-8

Typesetting by www.beamreachuk.co.uk

For Nikita, Monstrie's best human friend.

MONSTRIE AND MUM

Once upon a time, there lived a little monster. His name was Monstrie, but he wished it was something else – like Jean-Clawed or Frightderick or Roarmeo. *With cool names like those, you could conquer the Monsterworld!* he thought. *With a name like Monstrie, you could only ... well ... sigh.*

So, he sighed about that, and about the tusk-mittens. You see, whenever Monstrie went out for a walk, his mum would put little woollen mittens on his tusks to stop him from catching a cold.

"Ouch! Prickly!" Monstrie complained.

"Nonsense, dear. There are no nerve-endings on your tusks," his mum insisted.

Monstrie hated going out in tusk-mittens. Firstly, because they flew off whenever he went down the slide. Secondly, because they ruined his reputation.

"Only babies wear tusk-mittens!" Sabretoothie sneered at him across the playground. It was mortifying.

Sabretoothie had it easy. He had perfect parents who let him watch TV in the evenings. Monstrie's mum was much more strict. "All we ever see on TV is roaring and biting. That's not something little monsters should watch!" she would say.

To make matters worse, she didn't let Monstrie eat any sweets. None at all! Because sweets are bad for the tusks. *But good for the soul*, Monstrie thought. He stashed chocolates in a special, very secret, hiding place: in the corner of his room, behind the sofa, under the carpet. Whenever his mum went out to work, Monstrie ate the chocolates in secret.

Unfortunately, Monstrie's mum only worked once a week. She was a part-time receptionist at the Museum of Monstrous Culture. So, Monstrie would save up a giant heap of chocolates. As soon as his mum closed the door behind her, he would gobble up the entire stash and get a huge tummy ache. When his mum returned, it was always the same: Monstrie lying on the carpet, achy and miserable, in a tell-tale pile of chocolate wrappers which rustled like colourful autumn leaves. His mum would put him on a healthy diet: boiled meat and rice – nothing sweet! His tummy felt better, but his heart sank.

Once, Monstrie complained about it to his best friend, Gorynych, who had three heads and was therefore very brainy.

"Your mum's a tyrant!" his friend declared.

"But what can I do about it?"

"Well … sooner or later, all tyrants are brought down," said Gorynych.

Monstrie didn't really understand what his friend meant. Gorynych loved to read, and he used a lot of grown-up words.

"Your mum must be stopped!" he explained. "Or else she'll make you live your whole life without sweets and cartoons!"

"But how can I stop her?!"

"You need to scare her off! Then she'll run away – and you'll never have to wear tusk-mittens ever again!"

"But how do I scare her off?"

"Well, think! You're a monster, after all! Scaring should be what you do best."

"I'm a little scared to scare Mum off," Monstrie admitted. "She might punish me for it."

Gorynych rolled his eyes (all three pairs of them). "Are you a fearsome fiend, or a doormat?" he asked.

"Well, I certainly don't look like a doormat," Monstrie said thoughtfully.

"If you don't do it now, she'll never leave you alone," Gorynych added firmly. "Wait until you start school! Everyone will laugh at those silly knitted tusk-mittens!"

Monstrie gulped. Clearly, there was no choice. He had to scare his mum off … before it was too late.

***

"She mustn't recognise you, or she won't get scared," warned Gorynych.

Monstrie put a large paper bag over his head. Gorynych painted a scary face on it, then glued some wooden sticks on top of it, like horns.

In his costume, Monstrie was utterly unrecognisable and definitely terrifying.

That evening, when Mum came home from work, all the lights in the house were out.

“Monstrie!” she called out. “Are you reading in the dark again? Don’t strain your night vision!”

As she fumbled around for the light switch, Monstrie jumped out at her. “GRRRRRRR!” he growled loudly. (Actually, he couldn’t roll his Rs properly, so it sounded more like “GLLLLLLLL”.)

To his surprise, Mum burst out laughing.

“What’s this? Are you rehearsing a play for school?” she asked with a smile. “That’s a cool costume. But remember: cows don’t growl – they moo.”

"I'm not a cow!" said Monstrie, offended.

"Then why are you wearing horns, sweetie?"

"I was trying to scare you off ..."

"You – what?!"

"Nothing. I think I'll go for a walk," muttered Monstrie quietly.

"Don't stay out too long. And put on your tusk-mittens!" Mum said.

***

Monstrie wandered sadly over to the playpark.

"How did it go? Did she run?" asked Gorynych.

"It didn't work," sighed Monstrie. "What kind of a monster am I, if my own mother isn't afraid of me?"

"Never give up!" his friend comforted him. "Maybe we could ask Sabretoothie to help out? Maybe he could scare your mum off?"

Monstrie didn't reply, because suddenly he saw something very odd and suspicious. A big van with two ugly monsters had stopped near the entrance to his house! Monstrie instantly nicknamed them 'Bony' and 'Giant'. Bony was lanky and gawky. Giant was burly and huge. Both monsters seemed incredibly shady.

Bony sat whistling at the steering wheel. Giant wound down his window and stared right into the windows of Monstrie's flat. A fake gold fang glinted in his jaws.

"Uh-oh! Who's that?" whispered Monstrie in alarm.

"Someone who's definitely good at scaring his mum," muttered Gorynych.

"Why are they looking through the windows of my flat?!"

Just then, Monstrie's mum came out. She was carrying a shopping bag and whistling a happy tune. Monstrie knew she would be heading to the supermarket. Suddenly, Giant jumped out, grabbed her, and shoved her into the back of the van!

Monstrie's heart nearly stopped.

"Let's go – quick!" hissed Giant to his scrawny accomplice.

Monstrie made a dash for it, but he was too late – the van was already moving.

"Stop!" Monstrie shouted at the top of his lungs. He imagined that he would never see his mum again ... never again hug her, or cuddle up against her warm fur. Oh no!

Monstrie ran after the van as fast as his little paws could carry him. He stumbled and fell, grazing his knees, but got up and ran on. The van stopped at a crossing. Monstrie sprinted and climbed onto its roof.

***

The van was driving further and further away from Monstertown, passing open fields, forests and sleepy villages, all wrapped in a woolly blanket of white fog. It wound its way along the twisty road, throwing Monstrie this way and that as he clung to the edge of its roof.

Finally, they stopped by a dark, forlorn house with broken windows. Monstrie jumped down quickly and hid behind a clump of nettles.

Giant and Bony got out of the van and went round to the back. Monstrie's mum was banging on the door.

"Get her out!" ordered Giant.

"Are you sure?" Bony shifted nervously.

"Don't be such a baby! We'll scare the living daylights out of her and she'll tell us everything – all the passwords and codes," sneered Giant, reaching for the door of the van. "There are so many precious paintings in that Museum of Monstrous Culture! It's the jackpot!"

"And what if she won't talk?" Bony asked, hesitating.

"I can make anyone talk. Even dragons!" Giant guffawed, flashing his sharp golden fang.

Oh no! thought Monstrie, trembling behind the nettle bush. *They're burglars. They've kidnapped my mum to get inside the museum!* He was very scared, and felt as if his heart had dropped right down to the tip of his little tail. *I have to save her!* he thought. *But what can I do?!*

He remembered what Gorynych had told him: "You're a monster, after all! Scaring should be what you do best."

Monstrie wasn't very good at scaring, but there was no other option. He plucked a bunch of nettles.

Giant pricked up his ears and looked about.

"There's somebody there," he growled, nodding towards the nettle bush.

"Maybe it's a chicken," gabbled Bony.

"The only chicken here is you!" snapped Giant, setting off towards the bush. Little Monstrie's tiny heart was all aflutter, like a butterfly trapped in a glass jar. He jumped out right in front of Giant and whipped him on the nose with the nettles.

"GLLLLL! Let my mum go!" Monstrie growled for all he was worth.

Giant let out a howl, more from surprise than from pain.

"You little brat! Just you wait till I get my claws on you!" he hissed.

Little Monstrie stood firm, fearlessly whipping Giant with the nettles, but Bony ran up and grabbed him by the scruff of the neck.

"I've got him, boss!"

"Great! Now I'm going to swallow him up, so he won't get in our way!"

Giant opened his huge jaws with their sharp golden fang. Little Monstrie squeezed his eyes shut. *Bye, Mum! Forgive me for being so useless and unscary!* he thought, trembling with fear.

Just then, something incredible happened! Giant suddenly turned pale, as if he had seen a ghost, and staggered backwards – right into the stinging nettles! Bony let go of Monstrie and rushed after him with a terrified scream.

"Ouch!" shouted the baddies, hopping up and down as the nettles stung their paws. Instead of stopping, they backed away even faster, looking at Monstrie in horror.

"Have pity! Don't hurt us, O mighty creature!" cried Bony.

"Please … we were just kidding … we didn't really mean it!" Giant chimed in.

"Are you talking to me?!" said Monstrie in surprise. Suddenly, he realised that they were talking to somebody behind his back …

Monstrie turned around and froze. Behind him loomed a fearsome creature – one that he'd never seen before.

It looked like a giant puffball.

It suddenly growled so loudly that both gangsters ran for their lives. Free at last, Monstrie rushed to the van to let his mum out. But the van door was open, and she was gone!

In tears, Monstrie glared at the creature.

"Where is my mum?" he shouted. "What have you done with her?!"

Instead of replying, the creature swept little Monstrie up in its paws. Monstrie squeezed his eyes shut in fear, but then lifted an eyelid. The fiend was cuddling him gently. It began to deflate, like a globefish, and suddenly Monstrie recognised his mum!

"Mum! Is that you?! I didn't think you could be so frightening!" he gasped.

Completely un-puffed, his mum was no longer scary in the least. She was just like she always was – smiling and kind.

"When my baby is in danger, I puff up with rage! And then I'm fearsome!" she explained with a laugh.

“I’m sorry I tried to scare you off!” said Monstrie as he buried his little snout in her fur.

“You silly thing,” his mum said as she comforted him. “You’ll never scare me off – it doesn’t matter how hard you try. I’m your mum, after all.”

Little Monstrie took his mum by the paw, and they went home. That evening, she made an exception in her strict parenting rules. They shared a chocolate bar and even watched TV together (although not for very long).

PAYBACK TIME

When little Monstrie started school, he learnt that he was an outsider. That's what Sabretoothie called him. Monstrie didn't fully understand why. Perhaps because he'd rather be outside than in school?

During lessons, he often gazed out of the window and wished he could fly. He imagined how he would fly up to the window of the classroom, flapping his long ears like wings. The other students would freeze in amazement. The teacher would drop her pointer and gasp, "This can't be happening!" But he would open the window and fly out into the courtyard. He would rise up higher and higher until the tiny houses, trees and cars down below looked like scattered toys.

“Monstrie! You’ve got your head in the clouds again,” said Mrs Clawhuge, the Monster History teacher, bringing him back from his daydream.

How does she know I’m thinking about the clouds? Monstrie wondered to himself.

“I’m a kikimora. We’re all mind-readers,” the teacher explained, instantly reading his thoughts. “I always know when you stop listening!”

Little Monstrie sighed. Oh, how he wished he could escape the classroom – if only in his dreams!

***

Monstrie’s least favourite subject was Monster Physical Education, in which little monsters were taught how to play sports, run fast and growl loudly. Monstrie didn’t like running and often mixed up the rules in games. But the growling was the worst.

“Growling is an essential skill for any monster!” announced Mr Dragonetti, the Physical Education teacher, in the first lesson. “Let’s start training! Who’s first?”

Monstrie quickly hid behind his best friend, Gorynych, who was chubby and therefore perfect for hiding behind. But you can’t fool an old dragon. Mr Dragonetti squinted and pointed his sharp claw right in Monstrie’s direction.

“You! I can see your ears! Out you come!”

Monstrie shuffled to the blackboard.

“On your marks! Attention! Growl!” cried the teacher.

Monstrie tried, but instead of “GRRRRRR”, it came out as “GLLLLLLL”. Monstrie couldn’t roll his Rs properly,

especially when he was nervous. The other students fell about laughing.

"How did they ever let him into school?" Sabretoothie sneered. "He doesn't play pawball. He can't growl. He's no monster – he's an oddball!"

"What does that mean?" Monstrie whispered to Gorynych, who liked to read and so knew all the words.

"It means you're not like everyone else," his friend explained.

Monstrie was very offended. His ears drooping sadly, he wandered off to his painting lesson.

***

Once he was painting, Monstrie cheered up a little. Oh, how he loved to paint! He had even invented a new art style called *im-paw-ssionism*. Monstrie would spread a sheet of paper on the floor, dip his paws into the paint, and then walk all over the paper to draw a picture – the sun, some flowers, his mum ...

"How unusual! Unique! Original!" the Art teacher gushed in admiration. But Monstrie didn't enjoy her praise. "Even *she* thinks I'm an oddball," he sighed.

During break time, some of the little boy monsters liked nothing better than to frighten the little girl monsters. The bullies would hide behind a door. Then, when a little girl walked by, they would jump out on her and growl loudly. The girls would flinch in fear and step on their own tails. Monstrie felt very sorry for them.

“Tigeressie, watch out!” he once warned a girl he was friends with. She turned around, saw Sabretoothie, and ran away. The bully snapped at Monstrie, “How dare you get in my way! Weirdo! Oddball!”

After that, Sabretoothie lost interest in bullying the little girls and took to bullying Monstrie instead: in the changing room, in lessons, during break and even in the cafeteria.

Once, when Monstrie was buying a salad, Sabretoothie scoffed: “Real monsters eat meat! And you’re eating grass like a rabbit! Ugh!” The other kids in the line giggled. Poor Monstrie was so upset that he forgot all about his salad and went hungry for the rest of the day.

“This is wrong! We’ve got to teach Sabretoothie a lesson,” sighed Gorynych.

“But he always skips lessons ... It would be very difficult to teach him anything,” Monstrie observed.

“I’m not talking about school lessons! We must teach him some manners. In short, it’s payback time!”

“What’s payback?”

“Work it out for yourself! Why should I have to explain everything?!”

Gorynych turned his back, indicating that the conversation was over. Monstrie sighed. His best friend knew so many clever words that he was very difficult to talk to.

I wish I had a special Gorynych dictionary, thought *Monstrie, to translate his words into ones I know!*

***

That evening, over dinner, Monstrie asked his mum, "What does 'payback' mean?"

"Where did you hear that word, my little one?"

Monstrie didn't want to tell her about Sabretoothie. "Er … it was just something that came up … in the cafeteria when I was buying a salad …" he mumbled.

"Ah …" Mum smiled. "It's very simple. When you buy a salad, you give the cashier ten monster coins, right?"

"Yep."

"And one salad costs only five. How much money should the cashier give you back?"

Monstrie worked it out quickly. "Five monster coins."

"Exactly! So that's paying back the change: the difference between the money you give the cashier and the cost of the salad. Now do you understand, dear?"

Monstrie nodded. He understood in principle. But he didn't really understand how change could save him from Sabretoothie. He wanted to ask Mum all about this, but didn't. Why should he tell her that he was being bullied at school? *The less Mum knows*, he thought, *the better she will sleep. That's a fact.*

"Is everything alright, my little one?" Mum asked.

"Yes!" Monstrie lied. "Good night, Mummy!" he added quickly. "Sleep well!"

***

The next day, Monstrie and Gorynych were buying ice cream in the cafeteria. Sabretoothie watched them wistfully – his parents had forgotten to give him lunch money, and he was very hungry. He had asked everyone to buy him some food, but nobody would.

"That'll teach him a lesson!" snorted Gorynych. "If you're a bully, nobody will help you when you need it!"

Sabretoothie heard this and yelled back at Monstrie and Gorynych so that everyone could hear.

"Well, I don't care! I don't want ice cream anyway! Real monsters don't eat sweets! You're not monsters – you're wimps! There's no place for you in our school!"

Monstrie and Gorynych exchanged glances.

"Pay him back," whispered Gorynych. "It's now or never!"

Monstrie was puzzled. He couldn't understand how giving the change to the bully could save them from bullying, but he decided to trust his best friend. He shrugged and gave Sabretoothie all the money given back to him by the cashier. The bully bared his teeth even more. "What's this?!" he said. "I don't need your pity!"

"It's not pity – it's payback!" shouted Monstrie and hurried away.

Gorynych ran off too – just in case.

***

Monstrie and Gorynych ran down the school corridor as fast as their paws could carry them.

MENU:

"Stop!" shouted Gorynych, gasping for breath. "I've lost all my glasses!"

Gorynych had three heads. Two of them needed glasses; the third one had perfect sight, but had to wear braces. "Life's never perfect," he would often complain. "If your sight is good, your bite is bad!"

Gorynych caught his breath, picked up both pairs of his glasses, and cried: "What was that all about? What have you done now?"

"I paid Sabretoothie back, like you said!" muttered Monstrie.

"That's not what I meant! Payback is an expression! It means to answer back – insult for insult, blow for blow!"

"But I don't want to insult anyone ..."

"Sabretoothie is a bully! The only way to deal with him is to show your strength. Instead, you gave him money and ran away like a coward."

"You ran away too," whispered Monstrie warily.

"Only to support you!" hissed Gorynych. "Now, we're done for. Sabretoothie will grind us into dust!"

***

Gorynych was clever, and his predictions usually came true. So, the next day, Monstrie did everything he could to keep out of Sabretoothie's sight. He entered the school by the back door and didn't even go into the corridor during break.

Towards the end of break, Sabretoothie barged into Monstrie's classroom. He walked about, looking under the

desks and into the teacher's cupboard, but he couldn't find Monstrie anywhere.

"Hey, furryheads! Have you seen Monstrie?" he asked the little girls, who were sitting at their desks. They shook their heads in reply. Sabretoothie noticed that the curtain on the window was twitching, as if somebody behind it was also shaking their head.

"Who's that, there?"

"The wind," replied Tigeressie confidently.

"The wind ..." murmured the curtain.

Sabretoothie rushed to the window and pulled the curtain to the side. There, trembling with fear, stood little Monstrie.

"Aha! Gotcha!"

Monstrie cowered in the corner.

"Please don't grind me into dust!"

He shut his eyes and imagined the teacher handing over a bag of dust to his mum in place of her son.

"Monstrie, what on earth do you mean? I'm looking for you to pay you back!"

Sabretoothie took five monster coins out of his pocket and handed them to Monstrie.

"Thank you," said Monstrie with a polite smile.

"Thank *you*. I had no lunch money yesterday," admitted the bully. "If it hadn't been for you, I'd probably have died of hunger!"

"But why didn't your friends help you out?" asked Monstrie in surprise.

"Because he doesn't have any," snorted Gorynych.

Sabretoothie was hurt. "Be quiet, geekheads!" he snapped. "Or I'll chew up all your glasses!"

"No, don't do that! That's bad for his eyes and for your teeth!" exclaimed Monstrie, shielding his best friend from the bully. Sabretoothie quickly backed down.

"Alright, alright. I'm not here to fight. I came to say thank you."

The bell rang, and Sabretoothie hurried off to his classroom. As he rushed out of the door, he turned around and called out, "Hey, Monstrie! Would you like me to teach you how to growl? Come to the playground after school! We'll practise growling and have a game of pawball."

Monstrie looked at Gorynych with great respect.

"You really are so clever! I paid him back – and now he's as nice as pie!"

"It wasn't the right kind of payback, but it worked anyway. A minor miracle!" observed Gorynych as he wiped both his pairs of glasses.

***

Sabretoothie kept his word and taught Monstrie how to growl. Monstrie even took to composing growl music. He and his friends wanted to start their own band. But that's another story ...

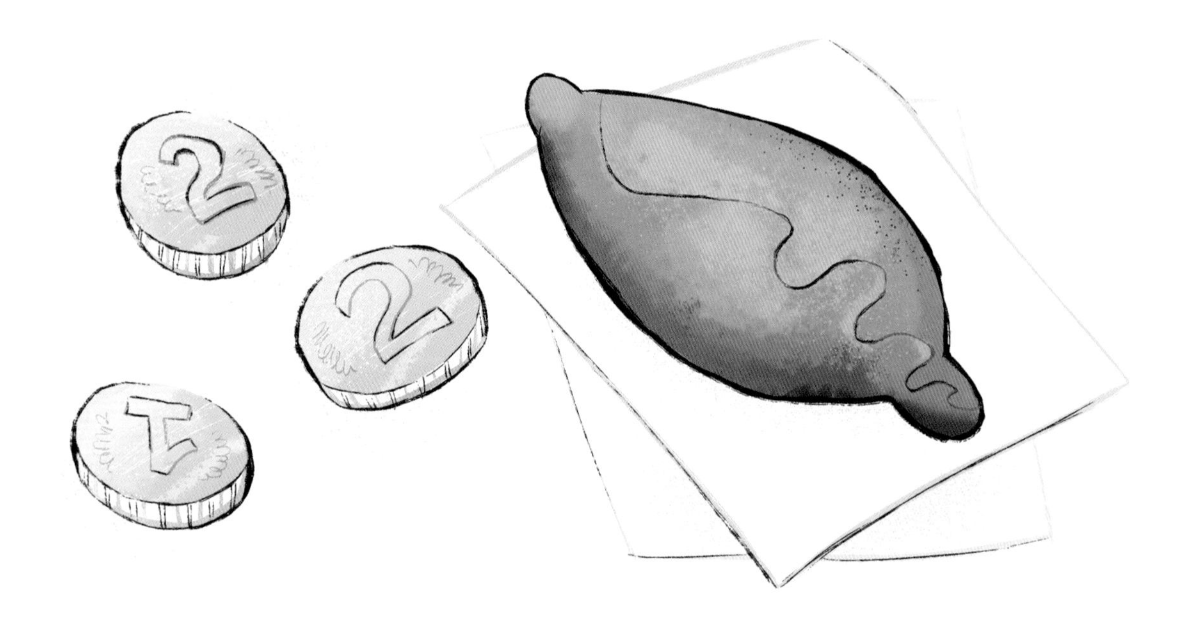

MONSTRIE INVESTIGATES

One day, Monstrie, Gorynych and Sabretoothie decided to start a band. Monstrie sang growl songs – he could growl with feeling about anything in the world: the sun, school, his friends, and his mum. He had real talent.

Sabretoothie was the drummer. He banged away to his heart's content on all sorts of objects: congas, bongos, wooden cupboards, metal buckets, cooking pots and pans – even the floor! It made for some interesting sounds.

Gorynych played the guitar and three wind instruments – the flute, the clarinet and the trumpet.

"Why are they called wind instruments?" Monstrie wondered.

"Well ... can't you guess?" snorted Gorynych.

"Maybe because when you play them, the room grows very windy?"

"No! Of course not, Monstrie! It's all very simple. They are wind instruments because you have to blow into them," explained Gorynych. He was also planning to learn how to play the xylophone with his tail – but that was something for the summer holidays.

***

One day, after school, Monstrie, Gorynych and Sabretoothie got together for a rehearsal. Monstrie growled so soulfully, Sabretoothie drummed so eagerly and Gorynych played with such gusto that all three of them felt very impressed with their own music.

"We're good at this," said Gorynych proudly.

"Let's give our first concert!" suggested Monstrie.

Sabretoothie thought this was a great idea. He leapt as high as the ceiling with joy. (His kind are very jumpy creatures.)

"Hurray! Who shall we invite?"

"Nobody," said Monstrie firmly.

Sabretoothie was so shocked that he stopped jumping at once.

"But who is the concert for, if we don't invite anyone?"

"For ourselves!"

"Monstrie, do you understand what nonsense you're talking?" sighed Gorynych.

"Yep! I'm talking very sensible nonsense. If we invite somebody to the concert, they might not like our music, right?"

"Right!" said his friends together.

“They might even laugh at us, right?”

“Right ...”

“So that’s why we’ll give the concert for ourselves. We definitely like our own music! We definitely won’t laugh at each other!”

“That’s very clever,” nodded Gorynych thoughtfully. “If we only invite ourselves to our concert, we will most definitely play to a grateful audience.”

“Whoopee! We’re giving a secret concert! I love concerts! I love secrets! Yay!” yelled Sabretoothie, clapping his paws happily.

***

The following morning, somehow everyone had found out about their ‘secret’. In some mysterious way, the whole school had heard about it.

“We’ll definitely be there!” the girls shouted to Monstrie during the break.

“Save a seat for me! Although, wait, I don’t need a seat! I’ll sit on my comfy new padded broomstick!” gushed the school’s custodian, Grandma Yaga, who was an elderly witch.

“What’s the dress code? Should I rent a tuxedo and a tail tie?” worried Mr Dragonetti, the dragon who taught Monster Physical Education.

On hearing all these questions, Monstrie was extremely surprised.

“How come everyone knows about our concert?!” he asked his friends.

“I’m guessing a certain furry and jumpy friend of ours spilled the beans ...” whispered Gorynych, glancing at Sabretoothie with disapproval.

“And I’m guessing someone couldn’t keep his three mouths shut!” snapped Sabretoothie, offended.

“Hey, don’t you fling accusations at me,” warned Gorynych, adjusting his glasses in a huff.

“Fine – I’ll fling something bigger and smellier! Like rotten cabbages!” growled Sabretoothie.

“Calm down, you two!” sighed Monstrie, pulling his friends apart. “What does it matter who let the secret out?”

“True. Words are like firebirds. Once they’re out, you can’t catch them!” mused Gorynych. “Now we’ll have to perform in front of the whole school!”

“Fine! I want to know if they like our music!” said Sabretoothie.

“I want to know too,” nodded Monstrie. He was very scared but very curious.

The bell rang, and they hurried off to their Mathematics lesson.

***

The Mathematics professor had a very wiggly tail. Whenever the respectable old monster was explaining some rule, he made gigantic wobbles and waggles with his tail – the way people make excited gestures with their hands. Sometimes the professor got so carried away that his tail would knock off his own spectacles – which was quite a spectacle.

Monstrie liked to watch the professor's tail. At the start of every lesson, Monstrie wondered what the tail might get up to this time. And it would always get up to something

different. Once, for instance, it tossed the class registration book out of the window just as the professor was about to enter a bad mark for Sabretoothie. It was hilarious! For this very reason, Monstrie loved going to Mathematics, or 'Tailematics', as he secretly called it.

But that day, Monstrie had the concert on his mind and never once glanced at the Mathematics teacher. This was unfortunate, as something awful happened during that class. Something very strange. Something that almost ruined Monstrie's reputation in the school.

It all began with the professor howling loudly, "Oh! Oh! My tail!" He jumped out of his chair and started running around the classroom, shouting out even more random and confusing words: "Horror! Rebellion! Outrage! Just you wait! All of you! To the headmaster's office! Straight away!"

The students looked at him, flapping their eyes, ears and tails. Nobody could understand why he was so upset. The professor motioned for all of them to gather around his chair.

Laid out on the seat were some sharp drawing pins! "Who dared to put THESE under my tail?!" he growled angrily.

Nobody said a word.

Who could have done something so awful ... surely not Sabretoothie! thought Monstrie in surprise. He glanced at Sabretoothie. But his friend was looking around, just as puzzled as Monstrie.

"So, nobody's owning up?" snorted the strict professor. "No matter, I'll find the culprit by experiment. Give me your backpacks! Quickly!"

Everyone put their backpacks on his desk.

"I'm now going to search your bags," said the professor coldly. "And if I find any drawing pins, I'm going to expel their owner from school!"

The students exchanged fearful glances. Monstrie, however, wasn't afraid at all. He was confident that he had no drawing pins. He was the first one to hand his backpack to the professor.

How startled he was, when the teacher triumphantly pulled a box of drawing pins from the side pocket of his bag!

"I didn't expect this from you, little one."

"That's not mine – I swear! Monster's honour!" said Monstrie, shocked.

"That's what you all say," the professor sighed. "Gather your things – we're going to the headmaster. And forget all about your concert. Pranksters don't deserve concerts!"

"Wait a minute!" said Tigeressie, who was a star pupil and Monstrie's friend. "How do you know that the pins on the chair came from that box?"

"A good point!" the professor conceded. He thought for a second and quickly found a solution. "That's easy to check. There are four pins on the chair, and on Monstrie's box it says there should be twenty of them. I'm now going to count all the pins in the box, and if there are four missing, he's the one who played the prank!"

The teacher counted all the drawing pins in the box. There were exactly four missing. Everyone was fully convinced that Monstrie was to blame.

***

"I didn't put those pins there. Cross my heart, paws and tail! May the dragon strike me down if I'm lying!" Monstrie assured his friends.

"Doesn't matter if it was you or not – our concert is never going to happen," grumbled Sabretoothie.

"I wonder how the pins got into my bag," sighed Monstrie.

"You were set up," said Gorynych. "It's all very simple. Somebody put pins on the professor's chair – and then hid the box in your bag to make it look like *you* did it."

"But why would anyone do such a thing?" asked Sabretoothie doubtfully. "Everyone loves Monstrie!"

"Not everyone, obviously. He must have secret enemies!"

"Oh no! Secret enemies are the worst kind! I'll never know who they are! And they'll get me expelled from school!" mumbled Monstrie in a panic.

"Don't worry! We'll catch them and punish them!" promised Gorynych.

"Yeah, we'll throw snowballs at them! And put a cactus on their seat! And take bites from all their sandwiches!" Sabretoothie had lots of ideas on how to punish Monstrie's secret enemies.

"But first, we need to find out who they are," said Monstrie. "So, we have to conduct an investigation, like the famous detective, Sherlock Bones!"

"Like who?"

"Sherlock Bones, the great human sleuth!"

"Actually, his name was Sherlock Holmes," the well-read Gorynych pointed out.

"Sherlock Bones sounds a monsterillion times better, though, doesn't it?" Monstrie replied.

***

Gorynych gave Monstrie and Sabretoothie a magnifying glass each.

"What do we need these for?" asked Monstrie.

“That’s the way it’s done. Detectives use magnifying glasses to search for clues and carry out surveillance.”

Monstrie and Sabretoothie started pointing their magnifying glasses at various objects. It was great fun to carry out the surveillance on the goldfish in the fish tank.

“Let’s focus, detectives! We have to come up with a list of suspects!” said Gorynych, tearing them away from the fish tank. “So, who could Monstrie’s secret enemy be?”

The friends racked their brains but couldn’t come up with anything. Whichever way they looked at it, everyone loved Monstrie – and nobody had a reason to set him up.

“I guess we make pretty hopeless detectives,” sighed Monstrie.

"But great musicians!" said Sabretoothie, tapping his tail on the floor and thinking up a new tune. "I'm a born drummer!"

"That's all very well, but if we don't find out who set Monstrie up by tomorrow, they'll cancel our concert and expel him from school," Gorynych reminded everyone gravely.

***

At home, Monstrie told his mum what had happened. She sighed and tutted for a long time. Then, surprisingly, she said, "I know who put the pins in your backpack!"

"I know too – my secret enemy!"

"No, dear. It was me!"

Monstrie almost bit his own tail in shock.

"You?! But why?!"

"You see, my little one ... when you told me that you didn't want to invite anyone to your concert, I got very upset. Because you can't have a proper show without an audience. So, while you were at the rehearsal, I made a poster about your concert and put it on the blackboard."

"But what does that have to do with the pins?" frowned Monstrie.

"Well, I pinned up the poster, and put the spare pins in your backpack."

"I see ... but how did they get under the teacher's tail?"

Mum shrugged.

"Maybe some bully tore the poster down and threw the pins on the teacher's chair?"

"Maybe," sighed Monstrie. "And now, because of that, I'm being thrown out of school ..."

"Just let them try!" fumed Mum. "You're a wonderful child! A little monster made of gold! I'm going to give that teacher a piece of my mind tomorrow!"

***

The next morning, Monstrie's mum marched into the classroom to teach the Mathematics teacher a thing or two.

"How dare you accuse my child?" she asked coldly.

"How dare your child hurt my tail?" retorted the old professor.

"He didn't hurt you! Monstrie's never hurt a fly in his entire life! He's the most kind and gentle little monster in the whole wide world!" Mum announced confidently.

Monstrie sheepishly flattened himself against his desk, watching the heated argument unfold. The more agitated the teacher became, the more he swished and swooshed his enormous tail. Eventually, the tail got so worked up that it knocked a pot of violets off the windowsill!

"Now look what you've done!" grumbled the professor to Monstrie's mum.

"I did that?! It was you!"

"You got me stressed! And when I'm stressed, I move my tail a lot! Please stop arguing with me before it destroys the whole classroom!"

"Wait a minute, Professor!" little Monstrie interrupted. "I think I know who put the pins on your chair ..."

The strict teacher turned to Monstrie and narrowed his piercing eyes.

"I know too – it was you!"

"No! It was your tail!"

"What do you mean, my tail?"

"When you explain things to us, you swish it a lot, right?"

"Yes ..."

"Well, then. It all makes sense. My mum pinned a poster up on the blackboard – and you accidentally knocked it off with your tail. That's how the pins ended up on your chair!" announced Monstrie triumphantly.

The professor paused. "I can't deny that this is a logical theory," he concluded thoughtfully. "Perfectly logical ..."

"There you are, then! That's the explanation!" smiled Monstrie's mum.

The old professor apologised to Monstrie for his mistake. When the lesson began, he turned to the class and said, "Children, do not rush to blame others for anything – your own tail might be at fault!"

***

That evening, Monstrie and his friends gave their first concert. Everyone in school loved the growling songs. Teachers and students alike growled them to themselves for a long time afterwards. It was a great success!

But everyone noticed that Monstrie's band had no name.

Monstrie thought a little and decided to call it 'Sherlock Bones'.

MONSTRIE GETS A SURPRISE

Little Monstrie had lots of interests. He loved daydreaming, painting, tickling and being tickled, playing pirates, watching cartoons, reading adventure books, growling songs, and lots more besides. But what he loved most of all was making plans. For instance, these were his plans for the weekend:

1) Brush my tusks.

2) Soak in the bath and play sea battles until the water gets cold and my ears go blue.

3) Eat porridge to make Mum happy.

4) Eat a chocolate to make myself happy.

5) Go to the playground and meet up with Gorynych and Sabretoothie.

6) Go on the swings and down the slide, play tag (no biting or getting bitten, because biting is <u>not</u> nice).

7) Go with Dad to the petting zoo and pet a unicorn.

8) Eat at least two sticks of candyfloss before Daddy sees.

Monstrie had a whole skyscraper of plans! However, plans may be one thing, but real life is quite another. On Saturday morning, Monstrie woke up early. He was in a terrible hurry. He wanted to carry out all his plans as soon as possible. But, to his horror, he couldn't even get out of bed!

"Are you okay, little one?" asked Mum, looking concerned.

Monstrie wanted to tell her that something strange had happened. Something that definitely wasn't in his plans! But all he could say was, "Ahem! Ahem! Ahem!" and, "Achoo! Achoo! Achoo!" He had hardly any voice at all and his whole body was aching – except for his tusks (because they have no nerve-endings).

He had fallen ill!

***

“Yes, this is bad,” said the doctor, a winged lion, shaking his mane. “Your son has a red throat and a fever.” Mum sighed and tutted. Monstrie also wanted to sigh and tut, but all he could utter was another “Achoo!”.

“Not to worry, though. There are some benefits to him getting so hot,” added the old doctor. “It means that he is fighting the infection. And, meanwhile, it will be warmer in the house. One little monster with a high temperature can do the job of two heaters! Anyway, he needs lots of rest. No running, jumping, or tail swishing. I prescribe hot chicken soup, three cups a day. And no school until you get well!”

These prescriptions made Monstrie feel even worse. He hated chicken soup and just loved to swish his tail.

“Alright now, I must get flying,” said the doctor as he opened the window. He was flying from one home visit to the next on his golden wings to avoid traffic jams.

Before flying out, he turned to Monstrie. “And no cartoons!” he said. “And no splashing around in the bath until you go blue! No sweets, either!”

Monstrie sighed.

***

It was hard being ill. Monstrie couldn’t go to school. He missed his friends a lot. His cough was going, and his temperature was coming down, but his mood was sinking as well. *Something needs to be done about this*, thought Dad.

One day, Dad came back from work seeming quiet and mysterious. He clearly had a plan of some kind. “Monstrie!” he called gently, holding both paws behind his back. “I know that things are tough for you right now. So here! I hope this will lift your spirits!” And from behind his back, Dad brought out a big box tied with a slender golden ribbon.

“Yay! A surprise!” Monstrie said, clapping his paws. He was feeling much cheerier already. He was about to open the present when suddenly – *Boom! Boom! Boom!* – a horrible knocking sound came from the box, as if there was a hurricane inside it.

Monstrie looked at Dad in alarm.

“Don’t be scared, Son! Open it! Be brave!” Dad said, winking.

Monstrie thought he heard somebody inside the box repeating Dad's words like an echo. "Open it! Be brave!"

It was scary opening this strange present. Squeezing his eyes shut, Monstrie tugged on the ribbon.

When he opened his eyes again, he found that he was hovering right under the ceiling – with Dad looking up at him in a panic.

"Looks like the present lifted me instead of my spirits!" exclaimed Monstrie.

Just then, Mum ran into the room. Looking up, she went pale.

"Let him go! Now! Stupid bird!" she screamed.

"Bird?!!"

Monstrie looked behind him and saw a long golden beak that was holding him by the scruff of his neck like a giant peg. Suddenly, the peg-beak opened, and Monstrie dropped straight down towards his terrified parents. He landed on some soft cushions that Mum managed to throw onto the floor.

"What have you done?! How *could* you buy him something like THAT?!" Mum said accusingly to Dad, hugging Monstrie close to her.

"At the pet shop, they said she was tame ..." muttered Dad guiltily.

Monstrie looked up. Swinging on the chandelier was a giant bird with big eyes, a golden crest and a colourful tail like a peacock's.

"Who's that?"

"That's your surprise ..." said Dad.

"It's nonsense!" said Mum.

"A surprise! Nonsense!" said the bird, copying Mum's and Dad's voices perfectly. She suddenly jumped down and landed on the sofa next to Monstrie.

"How *could* you buy him a firebird?!" vented Mum, still beside herself. "They're wild! They get up to all sorts of things!"

"All sorts of things!" agreed the firebird in Mum's voice, calmly cleaning her feathers. Up close, she looked quite interesting and not scary in the least.

"Dad, why does she copy our voices? Does she not have a voice of her own?" Monstrie asked in surprise, studying the wondrous bird.

"Of course she does. It's just that the firebirds are very shy. They only use their own voice to talk with those they truly love," Dad explained. "You see, the love of a firebird has to be earned."

"Well, we're not going to be earning it," said Mum. "Dad is going to return this dangerous creature to the pet shop right now."

"No, please, let's keep her!" begged Monstrie. "She doesn't look dangerous at all! She looks fun! It would be a pity to hand her back!"

“A pity to hand her back ...” the firebird repeated in a timid echo.

Mum looked sternly at the curious bird, at Monstrie, and at Dad, as if deciding the fate of all three of them. Pausing for a dramatic moment, she finally spoke. “Well then, what are we going to name her?”

“Yaaaaay!” cried Monstrie.

They were going to keep the firebird.

***

Monstrie immediately invited Gorynych and Sabretoothie over. He wanted to show off his new pet.

"Let's call her Rex!" suggested Gorynych.

"Nonsense! Rex is a dog's name!" scoffed Sabretoothie.

"Exactly! There are lots of dogs called Rex – but nobody has a firebird called Rex! It's going to be so original!"

Gorynych walked over to the firebird's cage and announced: "Hey, Rex! Would you please grant me a new backpack, top marks in Maths and a truck-load of jam buns?"

Monstrie looked at Gorynych in bewilderment.

"What are you mumbling over there?"

"I'm not mumbling – I'm making a wish. Don't you know that firebirds can make any wish come true?"

"Any wish? That's hardly ..." said Monstrie doubtfully.

“It’s a scientific fact!” insisted Gorynych. He turned to the firebird and added: “I also want a new scooter! And I want summer to last forever!”

The firebird stared at him blankly. Then she turned away and began cleaning her feathers just like any other bird.

“There, you see? She doesn’t know how to make wishes come true,” whispered Monstrie in disappointment.

“Of course she does! But she needs inspiration. Maybe my wishes don’t inspire her,” Gorynych sighed.

***

The mysterious bird settled in at Monstrie’s house and even got used to being called Rex, responding whenever Monstrie affectionately called her Rexie.

Each morning, at breakfast, Monstrie would let the firebird out of her cage. While he was eating his porridge, she would peck at some seeds. Monstrie couldn’t stand porridge, so he taught his new pet a trick: as soon as Mum’s back was turned, he would hand his plate to the bird. She would take it in her beak, fly up to the window, and quickly throw the porridge out.

“Finished already?!” Mum would ask, marvelling at his empty plate.

Monstrie would nod, and Mum would let him and Rexie leave the table.

After breakfast, they would set off for school. Monstrie would clamp his arms around the firebird’s neck, and she would lift him high, high above Monstertown. At first,

Monstrie was a little afraid of flying like that, but he quickly got used to it.

As the firebird flew past skyscrapers, Monstrie would peek through the windows of the upper floors and see the townsfolk eating breakfast, getting ready for work, grumbling and growling, watching the news, washing their tails, combing their manes and cleaning their fangs. “Hi!” Monstrie would shout, waving to them politely. Caught off-guard, the citizens of Monstertown would freeze and stare at the strange flying object in shock. It was such fun!

At school, when the orchard was in flower, the firebird would fly up to the apple trees so that Monstrie could pick a few twigs of blossom. When he landed, he would give the bouquet to his friend Tigeressie.

“Wow! You climbed the apple tree for my sake!” she would say in delight.

Monstrie would nod, and the firebird would keep his secret.

***

While Monstrie was in class, Rexie would wait for him in the playground. She behaved like a perfectly ordinary bird, jumping into puddles with the sparrows and chasing the pigeons. Sometimes she would creep up to the classroom window and knock her golden beak against the glass to remind Monstrie that she was there.

"Quiet, please!" the young science teacher, Mr Hickory Pine, would say in a strict voice.

"Quiet, please!" the firebird would repeat in the teacher's voice, quickly ducking out of view.

"Who said that?!" demanded Mr Pine.

"Who said that?" repeated the firebird, just like an echo.

Mr Hickory Pine came from an ancient and noble family of wood spirits. He held a very high opinion of himself and couldn't stand it when the students were noisy or – heaven forbid! – played tricks.

He would rush to the window in a fit of rage, looking for the trickster – but all he could ever see was a harmless spruce bush.

"To the headmaster's office! Now!" the furious teacher would boom at nobody in particular.

"To the headmaster's office! Now!" the bush would shout in reply.

"I bet there's some mischievous ghost hiding out there," Tigeressie would whisper in fear.

"Please, don't insult ghosts. They regularly visit my outstanding lectures, of course ... but they don't interrupt lessons," protested the teacher. "It's *not* a mischievous ghost – it's someone up to ghastly mischief! And I'm going to complain!"

"And I'm going to complain," the bush would mutter in reply.

Mr Hickory Pine could stand it no more. He ran out of the classroom and went to inform the headmaster about something 'outrageous and preposterous' – although he couldn't explain exactly what.

Monstrie, Gorynych and Sabretoothie giggled. They knew that it was just the firebird playing tricks.

***

When summer came, Monstrie and his friends went to the lake every morning. One day, they climbed into an old wooden rowing boat that they found on the shore. Monstrie tied a long rope to its bow. The firebird seized the rope in her beak and flew swiftly above the lake, dragging the boat behind her. Monstrie, Gorynych and Sabretoothie raced across the water at full tilt.

"Hold on!" Sabretoothie shouted.

"Hurray! We're flying to outer space!" Monstrie called.

"I'm scared! Slow down! Aaaahhh!" Gorynych cried out with all his three mouths at once.

Just then, the firebird drew a circle in the sky, and the boat turned over with a splash. The three friends roared with laughter as they landed in the water.

After a refreshing swim, Monstrie, Sabretoothic and Gorynych sunbathed. Whenever the sun got too hot, the firebird opened her wide wings above them like a fan, and they found themselves in a pleasant shade.

"I wish my parents would buy me a firebird too!" sighed Sabretoothie. "All I ever get is books. Most of them I can't digest! My tummy aches from all this literature!"

"You mean you eat books?!" asked Monstrie in disbelief.

"Well, of course!" nodded Sabretoothie. "Dad tells me literature is great food for thought, so I eat three volumes a day. I can't stand the sight of it any more! Yet I don't seem to have got any smarter. Yep, it would be much better if Mum and Dad gave me a firebird!"

"Monstrie, you're so lucky! Your parents rock!" Gorynych chimed in.

At times like that, Monstrie would give the firebird a big hug and whisper, "Rexie, you're my very best friend!"

"You're my very best friend!" Rexie would repeat joyfully in Monstrie's voice.

***

Summer ended and autumn arrived – all gloomy and slimy, like a sea-monster. Rain drummed on the windows. The sun-loving firebird began to brood. She stopped talking, lost her appetite, and refused to go outside.

"She's not used to our northern climate," Dad explained.

Monstrie had to go to school alone. At first, he missed Rexie, but then he got used to it.

When the winter came with its frosty days, clear skies, and snow as fluffy as a baby unicorn's mane, Sabretoothie started teaching Monstrie how to play *tail hockey* – a type of hockey where you have to strike the puck using your tail. To win in tail hockey, you need a long tail and a lot of spirit. Monstrie's tail left much to be desired, but he had plenty of spirit.

Monstrie got so keen on tail hockey that he spent all his free time on the ice rink, honing his skills. He hardly ever thought about the firebird. Rexie was now entirely in Mum's care. "I warned you he wouldn't take care of her!" Mum occasionally complained to Dad. "We should never have got her! Now she's a millstone around my neck!"

"A millstone around my neck!" Rexie repeated, staring sadly out of the window.

***

One evening, on returning home from the ice rink, Monstrie discovered something very strange. Mum was standing by an open window, covering her snout with her paws. Ice-cold wind blew through the curtains, and snow whirled in like a vast white swarm, swirling round and

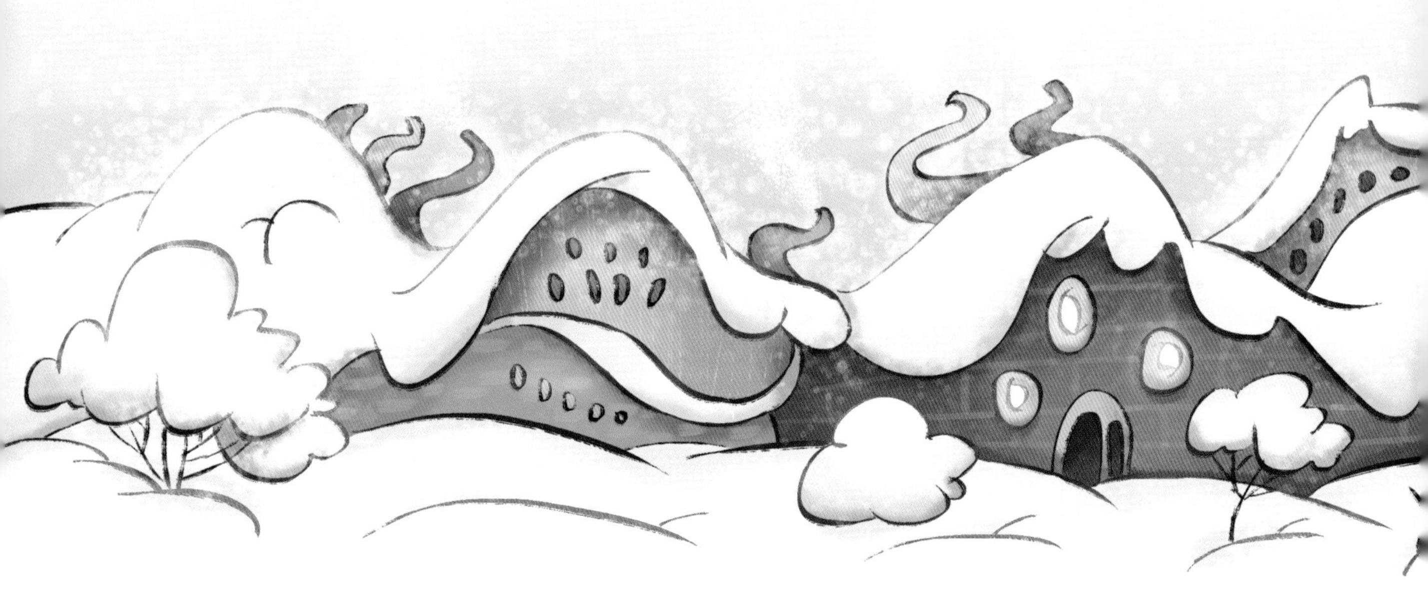

round, landing on the carpet, on the tablecloth and in Mum's tea ... but she was paying no attention.

"What's happened?" Monstrie whispered, sensing trouble.

Mum sighed heavily and wiped the tears from her eyes.

(That was no easy task because Monstrie's mum had two pairs of eyes: one on her snout and another on the back of her head. Thanks to this, she could always see what was going on behind her back – a very useful skill for bringing up little monsters.)

"I should never have complained about her. She was so cute, kind and gentle!" mumbled Mum, at last. "How's she going to survive now, out there in the cold, all alone?! She'll die! She'll perish!"

Monstrie noticed that the firebird's cage was empty. She had flown away!

“Rexie, come back!” called Monstrie desperately, running out into the snowy street.

“Monstrie, come back!” shouted Mum from the window. “Put a coat on, or you’ll catch a cold!”

He didn’t hear her. He could only think of getting his firebird back.

Monstrie ran all around the courtyard and then rushed off towards the lake, but Rexie wasn’t there. Soon night fell, and a blizzard started. The fierce wind buffeted and swayed Monstrie on frozen waves of snow.

He remembered that the firebird was very afraid of cold. She was probably terrified now, out on the street all alone – even more terrified than he was. He imagined that the snow had covered the delicate bird with its heavy white paw, and turned her into a block of ice. Or perhaps, fleeing from the snowstorm, she had flown into the house of some other little monster – a less kind and sensible one

– and he, instead of befriending the little feathery guest, had swallowed her up!

Losing all hope, Monstrie sat down on a bench near his house. The icy wind was lashing his little snout, and it was dark all around – but he had absolutely no desire to go home.

"Rexie! If you really can make wishes come true, please come back! I wish it! More than anything else in the world!" he shouted into the night, hoping that the firebird would hear him.

But instead, Dad heard him.

"Monstrie! There you are!" he said, sighing with relief. "Mum told me your firebird flew away."

"Yes," sobbed Monstrie. "I don't understand why ..."

Dad brushed the snow away with his tail and sat down on the bench next to his son.

"Well, actually, it's quite understandable. You became so used to her that you stopped playing with her and caring for her. Firebirds don't like that! But never mind – we learn from our mistakes, Son."

Just then they suddenly heard something truly magical – birdsong, warm and gentle like the spring sun!

"Why are the birds singing as though it's spring?" Dad wondered.

"Oh! Look!" exclaimed Monstrie, pointing upwards.

Hovering above them was the firebird. She was singing in her real voice for the first time!

"Rexie's back! My wish came true! Yay!" shouted Monstrie, beside himself with joy.

***

Mum knitted a woollen vest for the firebird so that she wouldn't be afraid of the cold. Monstrie started taking Rexie with him to the ice rink and taught her to play tail hockey. Instead of using her tail, the firebird would strike the puck with her powerful beak. She soon became an expert player.

Monstrie never forgot about his firebird ever again. He admired her every day, just like he had on the day she was given to him.

A LESSON IN SCARING

One day, a new teacher appeared in school. Or rather, his tusks appeared first. They were so long that wherever the teacher went, they would always appear before he did. His enormous paws with sharp claws would appear next, followed by the giant teacher himself.

He was so big that he had to squeeze into the classroom. He was so tall that his horns scraped the ceiling, and he always had to hunch his shoulders when walking along the school corridors.

Hunching your shoulders is a very bad habit, but nobody dared to tell this to the teacher – if he had suddenly decided to stand up straight, he would surely have brought the ceiling down.

"Good morning, young monsters, dragons, and other gruesome creatures!" said the teacher, staring at the students with eyes like red-hot coals. "My name is Mr Pompus Fright!"

Monstrie looked up and froze. The teacher's appearance was just as frightening as his name. Mr Fright was huge, like a mountain. His whole body was covered in coarse black fur – and in some places, moss. On his long, hooked nose, there grew a big toadstool.

"I will be teaching you the most useful subject in school: Scaring Basics," announced Mr Fright proudly. "Because, tell me, please, what is the most important thing in life?"

"Food?" muttered Gorynych with his middle head, while the other two secretly chewed jam buns under the desk.

"Wrong!" exclaimed the teacher, seizing him by the scruff of the middle neck. "Food is *not* the most important thing in life! So, what is the most important thing?"

"Mums!" Tigeressie shouted out confidently.

"No! Mums are not so important," frowned the teacher as he let go of the terrified Gorynych. "The most important thing in life is the ability to scare! Is everyone clear on that? Any questions?"

"I have a question," murmured Monstrie, timidly raising his paw. "Why do you have a toadstool growing on your nose?"

"What?!" exclaimed the teacher, staring right at Monstrie with his fiery eyes. "What did you say?!"

"I-I-I asked w-w-why you have a t-t-t-oadstool on your n-n-nose ..." stuttered Monstrie in fear.

"What a nerve! What outrageous cheek!" the teacher frowned. "Next you'll be saying that I have cobwebs hanging down my eyelids – or that I've got a piece of bog-

SCARI
BASIC

wood sticking out of my ear! Never once, in one hundred and forty years of my life, have I heard it said that I've got a toadstool growing on my nose!"

"But … surely you must have a mirror?" said Monstrie in surprise.

"Mirrors? Of course not! I never look in a mirror! Why do you think that is?!"

"Because you're not vain?" suggested Gorynych.

"No! Because I *can't* look in a mirror. As soon as I walk up to a mirror, I immediately smash it with my tusks! What an insult to suggest that a monster with big tusks like mine looks at himself in a mirror!"

The offended teacher planted his glasses on the tip of his nose (or rather, on the toadstool) and cast a stern glance at Monstrie. "I can see that you're very cheeky and ill-mannered! But, never mind – I'll sort you out! I'll take you in hand."

"Oh, no! Please, don't!" babbled Monstrie, hiding beneath his desk to stop the teacher taking him in hand. "I'm only a little bit cheeky, and I'm quite well-mannered! I was simply ... curious."

The teacher snorted as if Monstrie had said something else to insult him. Turning towards the other students, he asked, "Now! Who *else* thinks I have a toadstool on my nose?"

Nobody dared raise a paw.

"There, you see? You're the only one! The only one who thinks that!" declared Mr Fright in a hurt tone. "So, what does that make you?"

"A minority?" offered Monstrie quietly. (He was very proud that he knew the word 'minority'.)

"No! A liar!" announced the teacher. He grabbed Monstrie by the paw and led him out of the classroom.

"The same will happen to everyone who raises my hackles!" Mr Fright told the remaining students as he left, his coarse fur standing on end with rage.

***

The next day, Mr Pompus Fright gave each of the students a cage containing a tiny mouse.

"Let me introduce you. This is a laboratory mouse," he announced. "Does anyone know what we are going to do with it?"

"Be friends?" Monstrie asked hopefully as he examined his little mouse. It was tiny and white, with a small chestnut-coloured patch on its nose.

"What nonsense! Be friends with a mouse?" frowned the teacher. "No. We're going to scare it!"

"But ... why?" asked Monstrie in bewilderment.

"Because scaring a mouse is the simplest of exercises. Every monster should be able to do it! Right then, show me what you're capable of! Yes, you, you!"

Mr Fright pointed to Monstrie.

"Demonstrate your ability to inspire fear in this little critter!"

With that, the teacher took the mouse out of the cage and placed it on the desk. Monstrie really didn't want to scare it, but he was afraid to disobey Mr Fright once again.

"Glllll!" he growled timidly, trying to put on his most menacing look.

"Squeak!" answered the little mouse cheerfully. Instead of taking fright, it suddenly jumped up and caught hold of Monstrie's tusk.

"Argh!" shouted Monstrie in surprise. He tried to catch the mouse, but it was very quick and nimble. It hopped onto Monstrie's nose, ran up and down his tail, and then dived into his armpit.

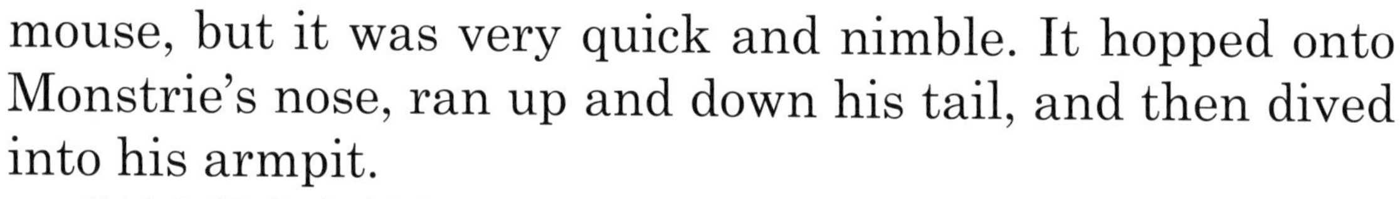

"Ah! Help! Ah! Get it off me!" shouted Monstrie.

"No, that's no good at all!" frowned the teacher. "What kind of a monster are you, if you're afraid of mice?"

"I'm not afraid of mice. I'm afraid of tickling!" Monstrie explained, trying to catch the mouse. It ran across his belly, tickling him with its tail. Suddenly, it peeked out of the collar of his sweater, jumped up and vanished, as if by magic!

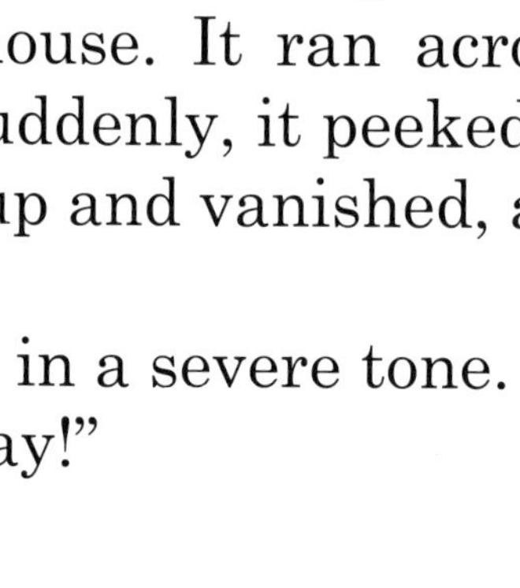

"Where is it?" asked Mr Fright in a severe tone.

Monstrie shrugged. "It ran away!"

"Well, then!" sighed the teacher. "Monstrie, you've failed the exercise and lost a school mouse! Sit down! You get an F! With two minuses!"

After the lesson, Monstrie left the classroom, his ears drooping sadly. He was very upset.

Suddenly one of his pockets started moving, scratching and squeaking. And there was the little mouse, shyly peeking out!

***

Monstrie hid the mouse in a shoe box under his bed so that Mum and Dad wouldn't find it. He made some small holes in the box so that the mouse could breathe, and a tiny little window so that it wouldn't be bored.

Late that evening, when his parents were asleep, Monstrie let the mouse out and began to practise scaring it. First, he rehearsed in front of a mirror, putting on a very scary snout.

There we are! I'm as good as the other little monsters! I'm quite fearsome. I'm pretty monstrous! he thought, looking at his reflection. *I'll really put the fright into that mouse, and get an A in Scaring!*

Determined, he turned towards the little mouse and growled at it in a whisper (so as not to wake Mum and Dad). Not scared in the least, the little mouse went and jumped into a bowl of biscuits.

Ah! Perhaps, that's the problem! It's hungry! Maybe it can't get scared on an empty stomach! thought Monstrie.

He sneaked into the kitchen and brought back some cheese, nuts and crisps. The food was five times bigger than the mouse, but it ate everything, right down to the last crumb.

“Right. Now you’re full up, you have to start getting scared, like you’re supposed to!” Monstrie said firmly to the mouse. “Surely I haven’t fed you for nothing?”

“Squeak!” said the little mouse, yawning.

Monstrie growled again, trying to look as fearsome as he could – and finally, it seemed to work! The mouse suddenly dropped down, closed its eyes, and didn’t make another sound.

Aha! I scared the living daylights out of it! thought Monstrie proudly, bending down to look.

The mouse lay motionless.

"Hey, Squeak! Why are you so quiet?" asked Monstrie, getting concerned.

The little mouse did not reply, and Monstrie suddenly felt very scared himself.

"Hey, Squeak! I'm sorry! I didn't want to scare you *that* much!" he murmured guiltily, cuddling the mouse in his paws.

"Zzzzzz! Zzzzzz!" was the reply.

The mouse was sound asleep!

***

From that day on, Monstrie had a little secret. It lived in a box under his bed. Monstrie stopped trying to scare the little mouse – no matter what he did, Squeak wouldn't get frightened. Feeding him, on the other hand, was very interesting: whatever Monstrie gave him – cheese cubes, apples, crisps, nuts, candles, even pencils – would be gobbled up with appetite.

Soon, Squeak had grown so much that he was no longer a little secret, but a big one. The shoebox became too cramped, and Monstrie had to move him to the wardrobe. There, Squeak spent his days sleeping and scratching.

Monstrie noticed that Squeak would scratch in a different way, depending on his mood. For example, when Monstrie was busy doing homework, the mouse made sad, bored sounds: *Scraaatch ... Scraaatch*. But when Monstrie finished his work and opened the wardrobe, the mouse greeted him happily: *Scratch! Scratch! Scratch!*

"Oh no! Mice in the house! I'll have to put down some mousetraps," sighed Dad, looking at the scraping wardrobe.

"It's not mice!" lied Monstrie.

"What is it then?"

"A ghost!"

"It's the first time I've seen a ghost stealing crisps, chewing candles and squeaking!" said Mum doubtfully.

"There's nothing strange about it. It's just that it's the ghost of a mouse!" insisted Monstrie, pushing his parents out of his room. He was afraid that they would discover Squeak and take him back to the school.

In the evenings, when his parents were busy making dinner and watching TV, Monstrie would let the 'ghost' out of the wardrobe. The mouse was happy to roam around and play. Over time, Monstrie taught him a few tricks like shaking paws, rolling over, fetching pencils and squeaking on command.

He was delighted with his little pet – yet one absolutely terrifying thought kept him up at night. *What if Mr Fright finds out that I've made friends with a mouse?! What will he do? He'll probably say that I'm the most hopeless student in school and throw me out! And he'll be right! What kind of a monster am I, if even a tiny mouse isn't afraid of me?!*

***

The school year flew by quicker than a firebird, and soon it was almost the summer holidays. But before school broke up, Monstrie had to pass his exams.

"Anyone who fails the Scaring exam will have to repeat the year!" announced Mr Fright. "You can't possibly go on to third grade if you don't know how to scare," he continued, looking directly at Monstrie.

"That's it! I'm done for!" gulped Monstrie. "I'm definitely going to fail the exam and I'll have to repeat the year! And in a year's time, I'll fail it again, and I'll have to stay on for a third time! Oh my! I'll be stuck in the second grade for all eternity, because I can't scare anyone and I'm a useless monster!"

After school, Monstrie took Squeak to the playground. The mouse dug out a burrow in the sand-pit while Monstrie poured out his heart.

"Why was I born so unscary and unthreatening?! If only I was as scary as Mr Fright! He's so enormous! With such long tusks! And a toadstool on his nose! Everyone would be afraid of me. Instead, I'm different to everyone else!"

"Squeak! Squeak!" said the little mouse in reply.

"Can't you say anything new on the matter?" sighed Monstrie bitterly.

"Squeeeeeeeak!" the mouse said even louder, peering at something behind Monstrie's back.

Monstrie turned around, and realised why the little mouse was so worried: coming straight towards them along the park path was none other than Mr Pompus Fright!

***

Mr Fright was strolling around the park at a leisurely pace, his giant body upright, his head proudly raised, and the spectacular toadstool on his nose glistening in the sunshine. The passers-by scattered and scampered away with screams to avoid his enormous tusks.

Monstrie looked at the teacher and couldn't believe his eyes. There was something wrong with Mr Fright – something very wrong! He was not walking alone: he was holding a leash, on which was slowly strutting … a large grey mouse. Monstrie was so shocked that he stood rooted to the spot until the teacher bumped into him.

"Oh! What are *you* doing here?" Mr Fright asked with surprise.

"I … l-l-l-live here," replied Monstrie, stuttering in fear.

"I live here too. So, you and I are neighbours then!"

"N-n-n-neighbours …"

Monstrie was so taken aback that he even forgot to hide Squeak, who fearfully leapt into his paws.

"What's that?" asked Mr Fright, squinting as he placed his glasses on his nose (or rather on his toadstool). "Monstrie! Why have you got a mouse in your paws?"

"And why do you have a mouse on a leash?!"

The Scaring teacher suddenly looked very scared.

"Don't tell anybody at school about this, okay?" he said sheepishly. "This is my little secret."

"A little secret – but a fat one too!" said Monstrie, examining the big grey mouse, which was sitting proudly beside Mr Fright like a faithful old dog.

"You see ... when I was as little as you, I could never scare anyone properly," the teacher explained reluctantly. "Instead of scaring my school mouse, I made friends with him ..."

"Oh! And that's the mouse?" asked Monstrie.

"No, alas! Puff the First passed away a long time ago," sighed Mr Fright. "Mice have much shorter lives than we do. But this is his descendant, Puff the Fourteenth!"

"But I don't understand! How come you couldn't manage to scare a tiny mouse when you are so frightening? You're my monster icon!"

"Well, truth be told, I'm not that scary," chuckled Mr Fright. "Just take a look at me! I'm awkward and clumsy – and I have a toadstool growing on my nose!"

"So you *do* actually know about the toadstool?"

"Yes! But I really don't like being reminded of it."

"Well, you definitely seem very frightening to me ... simply terrifying," confessed Monstrie.

"That's probably because you're only in second grade. Once you move on, you'll realise that I'm not that scary."

"But I'll never move on! I'll probably grow old in second grade," muttered Monstrie sadly.

"Why's that?!"

"Because I'll never pass your Scaring exam!"

Mr Fright shook his enormous furry head, scratched the giant toadstool on his nose and then suddenly asked: "Tell me, little friend ... what's the most important thing in life?"

"The ability to scare!" replied Monstrie confidently.

"Wrong! There is something *even* more important than that. They don't teach it in school, but I'm going to tell you anyway ..."

"Hope it's not the ability to growl! I'm even worse at that."

"No! The most important thing in life is to be yourself!" declared Mr Fright triumphantly.

Monstrie was baffled. "Well, how can I not be myself? I can't have three heads like Gorynych! I can't bounce on my paws as well as Sabretoothie! I can't be as blood-curdling and scary as you! All I can do is be myself."

"Now you're thinking!" smiled the Scaring teacher.

Mr Fright tousled the fur on Monstrie's head, put his mouse on his shoulder and went on his way – humming something softly to himself or, perhaps, to his tiny pet. And Monstrie suddenly felt that he was no longer afraid of the Scaring teacher at all ... despite his extremely sharp claws and huge tusks.

***

Finally, the day of the Scaring exam arrived.

"Now then, young monster ladies and gentlemen!" Mr Fright addressed the class. "Show me what have you learnt this year!"

The students fidgeted uneasily. Everyone was very nervous; Monstrie most of all. He was sure he was going to fail the Scaring exam.

"Come on now, young Scarers! Be brave! Who's first?" asked the teacher impatiently.

Tigeressie mustered some courage, and came out to the blackboard. She always liked to go first.

"I'm going to demonstrate the Great Griffin Mouse-Scaring Method!" she announced proudly.

While Monstrie was wondering why the Great Griffin needed to scare harmless little mice, Tigeressie growled at her lab mouse with all her might. The terrified critter jumped off the desk like a speeding bullet.

"Well done! As always!" exclaimed Mr Fright. He poked his long claw into an inkpot and drew a thick blot in the shape of the letter 'A' in the class register. Holding her head high, Tigeressie sat down at her desk.

And so it went on, one student after another, until all the students had passed the exam. All except Monstrie, who had hidden under the desk at the very back.

"Monstrie!" the teacher called, finally. "That's enough of being afraid. Come out and show us how well you scare!"

Monstrie had no choice. He went up to the blackboard, took Squeak out of his pocket, and placed him on a desk.

Only he did not attempt to scare Squeak at all. Instead, he gave him a friendly smile!

And at that moment something incredible happened.

Terrified, the little mouse dashed away from Monstrie as fast as his little paws could carry him. He ran across the walls, the desks, the ceiling, across the students' paws and tails, and even across Mr Fright's giant tusks, before hiding in the farthest corner of the classroom.

"Well, that was just ... excellent!" gushed the astonished teacher in delight. "Monstrie, what a surprise! I never thought you had it in you! That was exemplary Scaring! An A-plus! No – an A with three pluses!"

And the Scaring teacher drew an 'A' with three messy pluses (that looked more like starfishes) in the class register next to Monstrie's name.

***

"How did you manage to scare your mouse so easily?!" asked Tigeressie suspiciously after Monstrie had returned to his seat.

"That's something I'd like to know too," muttered Gorynych. "I spent the whole term working on my Scaring –

and you did nothing at all! Yet you got the best grade! What's your secret?"

"My secret is that I didn't scare him at all," admitted Monstrie honestly. "I just made friends with him. So now, if I ask him very nicely, he does me a favour and acts very scared. In fact, he can do lots of cool tricks! Here, watch this!"

Monstrie clapped his paws once and the little mouse rolled over.

Monstrie clapped three times and the mouse did a somersault.

"Look at that! That's *so* cool! I want a pet mouse too!" shouted the excited students, crowding around Monstrie.

"Quiet!" bawled Mr Fright. But nobody was listening to him. The students forgot all about Scaring. Everyone started teaching their mice to do tricks.

And so, Monstrie went to third grade. Squeak also went to third grade, because he enjoyed going to school much, much more than sitting in the wardrobe.

MONSTRIE GLOSSARY

Growl music – a popular musical genre involving growling.

Impawssionism – a style of painting in which the paws are used to paint pictures.

Pawball – a team sport in which the players use their back paws to strike a ball into the opposing team's goal.

Tail hockey – a team sport, played on ice, in which the players use their tails to hit a puck and score goals against their opponents.

Tusk-mittens – woolly caps placed on the tusks of little monsters in cold weather.

CAN YOU SEE MONSTRIE?
SCHOOL
CAN YOU SPOT A UNICORN?
WHERE DID
BONY AND GIANT
DRIVE TO?

WHERE DOES MONSTRIE LIVE?
CAN YOU FIND TEN FIREBIRD FEATHERS?
MUSEUM

AUTHOR

Maria Kabanova has won awards for her films and poetry. A UCLA film school graduate, she has written a blockbuster film and several TV shows. Writing children's books appeals to her youthful heart.

ILLUSTRATOR

Margarita Grezina has a talent for creating unique and adorable characters. "To me, the message is the most important aspect of the artwork. I enjoyed working on these fun and wise stories about little Monstrie!"

MARIA KABANOVA
ILLUSTRATED BY MARGARITA GREZINA
LITTLE
MONSTRIE'S
BIG
ADVENTURES